DUMPLING SOUP

by

Jama Kim Rattigan

Illustrated by

Lillian Hsu-Flanders

Little, Brown and Company

Boston New York Toronto London

For Grandma Yang

J. K. R.

For Aaron and Adriel

And with thanks to Sólrún Hafthórsdóttir
for her enthusiasm and patience

L. H-F.

First Edition

Library of Congress Cataloging-in-Publication Data
Rattigan, Jama Kim.
  Dumpling Soup / by Jama Kim Rattigan ; illustrated by Lillian Hsu-Flanders. — 1st ed.
    p.   cm.
  Summary: A young Hawaiian girl tries to make dumplings for her family's New Year's celebration.
  ISBN 0-316-73445-4
  [1. Family life — Fiction. 2. Cookery — Fiction. 3. Hawaii — Fiction.] I. Hsu-Flanders, Lillian, ill. II. Title.
  PZ7.R19386Du   1993
  [E] — dc20   91-42949

10 9 8 7 6 5 4

BER

Published simultaneously in Canada by Little, Brown & Company (Canada) Limited

Printed in the United States of America

GLOSSARY

ENGLISH

litchi	LĪ-chee (more common pronunciation in Hawaii), also LEE-chee	tree with a nutlike fruit

HAWAIIAN

haole	HOW-lee	white person, foreigner
hapuu	hah-POO-oo	tree fern
Kahala	kah-HAH-lah	amberjack fish; a town on the island of Oahu
Kaneohe	kah-neh-O-heh	Kane (of the) bamboo, a Hawaiian god; a town
Oahu	o-AH-hoo	gathering place; one of the Hawaiian islands
ono	O-no	delicious
Wahiawa	WAH-hee-ah-wah	place of noise; a rural town on Oahu
Waialae	WAH-ee-uh-lah-eh (to be spoken very quickly so syllables run together)	mud hen water; neighboring town of Kahala

JAPANESE

mochi	mō-chee	chewy rice cakes with bean filling
sashimi	sah-shee-mee	raw fish
sushi	soo-shee	raw fish with vinegared rice

KOREAN

jhun	chōn	food fried in egg batter
kimchi	kim-CHEE	spicy pickled vegetables
mandoo	muhn-DOO	dumplings
namul	nah-MOOL	seasoned vegetables
taegu	tī-GOO	seasoned shredded codfish
yak pap	yuhk pahp	sticky rice dessert with honey, dates, and pine nuts

PUBLISHER'S NOTE

In the fall of 1990, we held our first New Voices, New World contest, encouraging writers from diverse racial backgrounds to submit children's book manuscripts. Of the over five hundred manuscripts sent from all over the world, Jama Kim Rattigan's *Dumpling Soup* stood out as a story that simply yet eloquently captures the experience of a young Asian-American girl. The tale is about a young girl's efforts to make dumplings as well as her family has been making them for generations at their annual New Year's celebration. Aptly expressing a child's sense of pride in tradition and family, the story conveys the importance of honoring a mixed heritage.

Set in Hawaii, where nearly fifty different races are represented, *Dumpling Soup* is a rich mix of food, language, and customs from many cultures—Korean, Japanese, Chinese, Hawaiian, and *haole*. The distinct traditions and heritage of each culture are not forgotten, but play a vital part in this close-knit family's life and in the preparation and eating of their traditional dumpling soup. Today, when our country is faced with the challenge of creating one nation out of many peoples, we see a special place in children's literature for a story that fosters such love and respect for diversity.

Every year on New Year's Eve, my whole family goes to Grandma's house for dumpling soup. My aunties and uncles and cousins come from all around Oahu. Most of them are Korean, but some are Japanese, Chinese, Hawaiian, or *haole* (Hawaiian for white people). Grandma calls our family "chop suey," which means "all mixed up" in pidgin. I like it that way. So does Grandma. "More spice," she says.

This year, since I am seven, Grandma says I can help make dumplings, too. Everybody in my family *loves* to eat, so we have to make *lots and lots* of dumplings.

The night before New Year's Eve, Grandma, Auntie
Elsie, Auntie Ruth, and Auntie Grace come to our house
to work on the filling. My mother has bought great big
piles of beef, pork, and vegetables to fill the dumplings
and special dumpling wrappers from the Gum Chew
Lau Noodle Factory in Honolulu. Everyone brings her
own cleaver and cutting board and sits at the kitchen
table, chopping and talking, chopping and talking, late
into the night.

"Too much gossip!" says Grandma in Korean.
"Mince that cabbage! More bean sprouts!" It is her
recipe, so she is very picky.

"What about me?" I want to help.

"Tomorrow, Marisa," answers Grandma. "You can
help us wrap."

So tonight I watch Grandma mix everything in a big
metal pan—more tofu, more onion, more salt, more soy
sauce. My aunties keep working, and I fall asleep
listening to the *chop-chop* pounding, *chop-scrape-scrape*.
Later, when my mother wakes me up to go to bed, her
hands smell like garlic.

The next morning, I am the first one up. I wake up my brother, Hiram. Then together we tiptoe to my mother and father's room.

"Get up, get up! It's New Year's Eve! We have to go to Grandma's to wrap the *mandoo*."

"Not yet," my mother says with her eyes still closed.

"Please wait till the sun comes up," says my father.

But we are too excited to sleep. Today, everyone will be at Grandma's. We will see cousins we haven't seen all year, and we will stay up all night. Hiram will help my uncles with the fireworks. But best of all, I will learn to wrap dumplings for dumpling soup.

When we finally get to Grandma's, other aunts who live near Wahiawa have already started wrapping. All of Auntie Faye's dumplings are rectangles, and she lines them up like soldiers. Auntie Ruth pinches her dumplings along the edges to make them look fancy. Auntie Grace puts more filling in the middle than anyone else. "I like fat ones," she says.

"Okay, Marisa, these are for you." Grandma places a small stack of wrappers in front of me. My mother pushes her bowl of finger-dipping water closer.

I want to make good dumplings. I want to show my aunties. I try to copy them, but sometimes I put too much filling in the middle. Sometimes I don't put enough water along the edges. My dumplings look a little funny, not perfect like the ones my aunts have made. What if no one wants to eat them? I feel Grandma's hand on my shoulder and look up.

"*Cha-koo hae bo-ra*, Marisa." I don't understand all of Grandma's Korean, but I can tell by her face what she's saying: "Don't worry—keep trying."

Soon there are trays and trays of beautifully wrapped dumplings all over the kitchen. They look like hundreds of baby bottoms wrapped in diapers, powdered on the outside. Mine look a little sad, all different lumpy shapes. One by one, my mother tosses all of them into Grandma's biggest pot full of boiling water.

When the dumplings are cooked, they float up, wrinkled and shiny. Grandma calls my father for the official taste test. No one knows spices like he does. He bites into one of the cooled dumplings, chews slowly, and wrinkles his forehead.

"What, too *mae wo*?" ("Too spicy hot?") My mother is anxious. "*Seen gu wa*?" ("Not enough salt?") "Or *jaah*?" ("Too salty?")

He gobbles up the rest of the dumpling, smiling and nodding.

"Mmmm! *Ono!!* One more to make sure."

I watch the pot carefully for my dumplings. There they are! But some float up without their wrappers. And others look like they lost their filling. Grandma scoops all of them into a colander to cool.

"We'll eat your *mandoo* later," she tells me.

But I worry that they are bad *mandoo* and that no one will want to eat them. Is Grandma putting them away so they won't spoil the soup? Maybe it's bad luck to eat ugly dumplings on New Year's.

Before I can ask her, more relatives knock on the door. They come from far away, from Kaneohe, Kahala, and Waialae. Now Wahiawa, which means "place of noise" in Hawaiian, becomes a place of *big* noise.

I hold the screen door open for all the aunties carrying heaping plates of food. "Watch out! Coming through!" They bring homemade *sushi*, *jhun*, and *sashimi*.

Auntie Mori arrives last with a special treat: Japanese *mochi*. She says *mochi-ii* means "to stay in your stomach for a long time." *Mochi-zuki* means "full moon." The little cakes do look like white moons, and the sweet, chewy bites feel so good in our stomachs.

"*Mochi* help keep the family stuck together!" my Uncle Myung Ho says after swallowing seven in a row.

More cars drive up. Now they line the whole street. By six o'clock, Grandma's front steps are covered with big, medium, and little slippers, sandals, and shoes. So many Yangs!

New Year's Eve is the only night in the whole year we are allowed to stay up all night. Grandma told us that in Korea, if you fell asleep before midnight, your eyebrows would turn snowy white. But staying awake is easy for us. We never run out of games.

"Let's hug Grandma!" shouts my *haole* cousin, Maxie. This is our favorite game. We line up in front of Grandma. When it is my turn, I stretch my arms to reach around her bouncy, soft tummy and then rest my head against it. She laughs, and my head bobs up and down. My grandma is like a warm pillow.

Inside and out, everyone finds something fun to do. We play a game we can play only on New Year's: shoe store. We go to the front steps. "I'll be the shoe store lady!" shouts Carrie. The rest of us take turns trying on all our favorite styles.

"Do you have these gold slippers in size fifty and a half?" asks Maxie.

"Aren't these red high heels just *perfect* with my muumuu?" Alicia shows off.

After a while, all the slippers and shoes get mixed up and seem to be walking all over Grandma's yard. Since it has gotten so late, we really should pick them up. But we're too tired.

When it is almost midnight, we hear Hiram and the older cousins running to poke big sparklers into the grass.

"Somebody check the clock!" orders Hiram. Alicia presses her face against the screen door.

"Twelve minutes to twelve!" she yells. All of a sudden it is almost time, and everybody moves quickly.

From every corner of the house the Yangs come. Everyone finds a place to stand on the cool grass. All the cousins gather under the litchi tree. The babies rub their eyes and whine. My Chinese cousin, Helen, says fireworks scare away the evil spirits. We want good luck in the coming year. Grandma takes one last look around to make sure everyone is there.

For a moment, the only sound is the shush of the *hapuu* plants. "Good-bye, Old Year," I whisper.

Finally we count down the seconds till midnight: Five, four, three, two, one . . . .

"Happy New Year!"

Thousands of firecrackers explode, filling the sky with smoke. All up and down Grandma's street, there is popping and snapping. Our eyes water and our ears ring. Hiram and I run to light all the sparklers, then write our names in the night sky. Cousins, aunts, uncles, brothers, sisters, and friends hug and shake hands.

Finally, Grandma calls, *"Ppalli! Mo-gup-sida!"* Time for *dumpling soup!*

"If we eat first thing on New Year's Day, we won't go hungry for the rest of the year," my father reminds us. The table is set with deep bowls and big spoons.

"Eh!" says Uncle Myung Ho. "What kind *mandoo* this?" I quickly look in some of the bowls. Oh, no! Grandma has put one of my funny-looking dumplings in each!

"Must be the ones Risa made," says Hiram. "They look like little elephant ears."

Everybody laughs. My face feels hot.

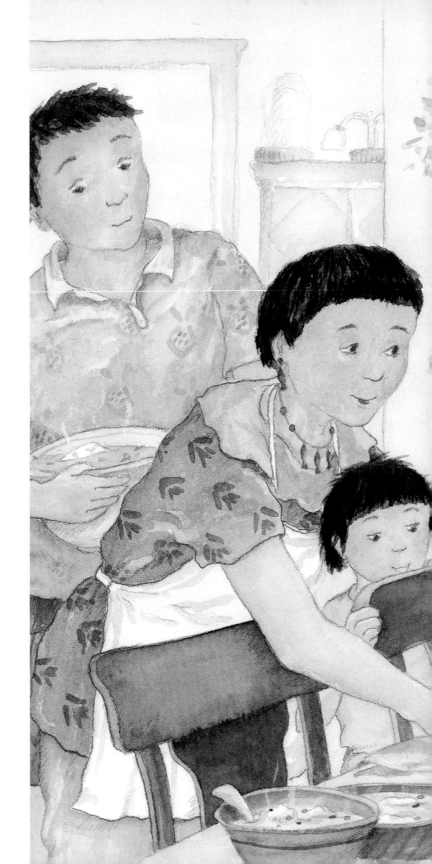

Uncle Myung Ho blows on his spoon and takes a bite. *"Ono,* Marisa! Delicious!"

Grandma walks over. Her bowl is full of my *mandoo!*

"I've been waiting all night to taste these," she says. "Here, have one." She puts another funny-looking triangle in my bowl.

We bite into our dumplings at the same time.

"Ai-go chŭm!" she says. "This is the best *mandoo* I have ever tasted!"

I finish my funny-looking dumpling. Mmmm! Grandma's right! It *is* good! The spices tickle my tongue.

"Who wants more of Marisa's *mandoo?"* Grandma asks. Everybody holds out his bowl. I hold out my bowl, too. More dumplings! More lip-smacking chicken broth! Warm, steamy, and delicious!

With our dumplings, we eat roast pork, three kinds of *kimchi*, spinach and bean sprout *namul*, spicy seaweed, *taegu*, boiled tripe, and octopus. Hiram and I love the Korean dessert we get only on New Year's: *yak pap*. He pulls off a chunk of the brown sticky rice mixed with honey, dates, and pine nuts and hands it to me. I lick every bit off my fingers.

"Your elephant ears sure tasted better than they looked!" he says to me.

I think about how much everyone liked the dumpling soup. Even my funny dumplings. Maybe it was because we ate them at Grandma's, all of us together.

"Next year," I tell everyone, "I will make even *better* dumplings."

I can hardly wait.

Hello, brand-new year!

My family — wearing new clothes for the new year!